CLASSIC FAIRY TALES

Ali Baba

Written by Barbara Hayes

Illustrated by Jesus Blasco

Library of Congress Cataloging in Publication Data

Hayes, Barbara, 1944-
  Ali Baba.

  (Classic fairy tales)
  Summary: A poor woodcutter discovers the hidden riches
of forty thieves, survives great danger, and makes his
whole family rich and happy.
  [1. Fairy tales.   2. Folklore—Arab countries]
I. Blasco, Jesus, ill.   II. Title.   III. Series.
PZ8.H325Al   1984   398.2'2''0953   [E]   84-11458
ISBN 0-86592-227-6

ROURKE ENTERPRISES, INC.
Vero Beach, Florida 32964

CLASSIC FAIRY TALES

Ali Baba

A long time ago there lived a poor woodcutter named Ali Baba. One day when he was working deep in the forest, Ali Baba heard horsemen riding toward him. At once, he climbed up into a tree to hide. He did not know if the strangers were friendly.

Forty men came riding by and Ali Baba knew then they were bad men. They were known to everyone as the Forty Thieves.

They stopped in front of a high cliff
and their leader stood in front of
the cliff. He said: "Open, Sesame!"

A door in the cliff swung open. Inside was a cave filled with treasure. The men went into the cave and unloaded sacks of gold from their horses. Then they rode away.

Ali Baba came down from the tree.

He stood in front of the cliff. He said: "Open, Sesame!"
Again, the cliff door swung open.
Ali Baba went inside, took some gold and went home.
Later Ali Baba went to the cave again and brought home more treasure. Soon, he was rich and he was happy.

Then Ali Baba's wife told the wife of Ali Baba's brother about their good luck.

At once Cassim, the brother, went to see Ali Baba. "Show me this treasure and tell me where you found it," he demanded.

Ali Baba told him.

Thinking that he would take some of the treasure for himself, Cassim went to the cliff. He said: "Open, Sesame!" Cassim went into the cave and picked up many bags of riches.

He was very happy and excited. He was so excited he forgot how the door could be opened from inside.

Poor Cassim was trapped in the cave. When the Forty Thieves came riding back, they saw Cassim's mules waiting outside the cave. "A stranger is here," cried the leader of the thieves. "Open, Sesame!"

As soon as the Forty Thieves saw
Cassim they rushed forward and
seized him. "A thief!" shouted the
thieves.

That night
Cassim did not
return home.
His wife became
worried. She went
to see Ali Baba.
"My husband has
not returned
home," she said.
"Will you go to
look for him?"

Ali Baba guessed
at once that
Cassim had gone
to the treasure
cave.
He went too and

found him there. Ali Baba untied
his brother and they went home.
However, the leader of the thieves
had followed them.

The Forty Thieves now knew where Ali Baba lived. They made a plan to get back their treasure.

The thieves' leader dressed as an oil merchant. He hid his men in large oil jars.

Late in the day the leader of the thieves went to Ali Baba's house with the oil jars.

He said he needed a place to stay.

He asked if he could stay in Ali Baba's home. Ali Baba and his wife agreed. They gave the thief dinner. The jars were put in the garden.

As darkness fell, a servant girl,
called Morgiana, found she
needed oil for her lamp.
It was too late to go to the shops.
"I will take some oil from those
big jars in the garden," thought
Morgiana.
When Morgiana touched a jar she
was surprised to hear a voice say:

"Is it time?" Morgiana was clever. She replied: "Not yet," in a deep manly voice and went on to the next jar. She found that only one jar was full of oil. All the other jars held a man.

Morgiana told Ali Baba. He came to listen at the jars. Ali Baba knew he was in great danger.

He suddenly remembered he had
seen the face of his visitor before.
It was the leader of the thieves.
"There are forty thieves in my
home," gasped Ali Baba.

Ali Baba called
his servants.
First, they tied
down the lids of
the thirty-nine
jars holding the
thieves. Then,
they seized the
leader as he
slept. They
emptied the oil
out of the
fortieth jar and
pushed the leader
inside.
Now they had
forty thieves in
forty jars.

Ali Baba took the forty thieves
hidden in their forty jars down to
the docks.

There, a merchant was about to
sail away to a far off country.

Ali Baba paid the merchant to take the forty thieves with him. They never returned.

So Ali Baba, his brother, Cassim, their wives and children were happy and rich for the rest of their lives. They gave gifts and help to all around them and their country became a happy place for all to live.

Test your memory

Read the story first. Then try to answer these questions.

Who is this girl? (Page 16) What happened when she touched a jar? (Page 16)

What words did Cassim forget? (Page 9)

Who rescued him? (Page 13)

After each question is the page number where you will find the answer.

Who told Cassim's wife about the treasure (Page 8)

Why did Ali Baba hide in a tree? (Page 4)

Why did she later visit Ali? (Page 12)

Who did he see ride by? (Page 4)

DATE DUE

D2B	m5B		
OCT 8	DEC 17		
P.5A			
OCT 12			
APR 2			
APR 05			

$9.25   #4076

398.2   Hayes, Barbara.
H
         Ali Baba.

601042   09067D